I0764782

Visit the author's Web site at

www.johnpender.net

Seven Days of Terror

This book is a work of fiction. Names, characters, places, and incidents are products of the author's imagination and are used fictitiously. Any resemblance to actual events, persons living or dead, or locales is entirely coincidental.

Copyright © 2009 by John Pender

All rights reserved, including the right to reproduce any portion of this book in whole or in part in any form whatsoever.

For reproduction permissions, please contact:

Pender Design Group LLC
attn: Permissions
P.O. Box 218
Winder, Georgia 30680

ISBN: 978-0-578-01944-4

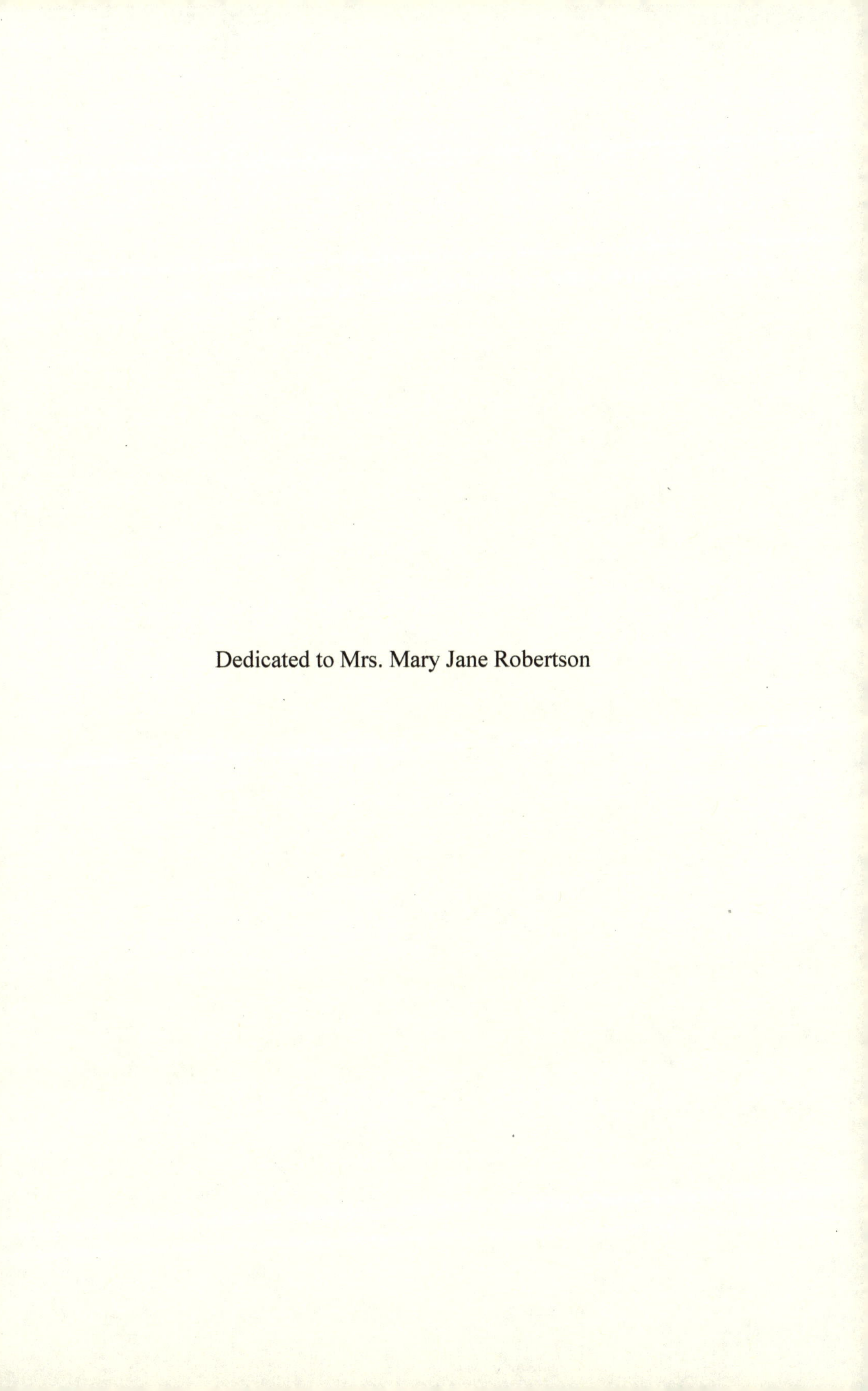

Dedicated to Mrs. Mary Jane Robertson

Special Thanks to Julie Bosche

*high school classmate, editor, friend,
and fellow horror movie aficionado*

I only wish our paths had crossed again sooner.

Contents

Foreword

On Inspiration

My inspiration for this book came from another book I recently picked up at a local bookstore called *100 Hair-Raising Little Horror Stories.* In it are, yes, one hundred little horror stories that are just the right length to read from start to finish during your average lunch break.

It's kind of refreshing being able to start anew each day with a different story. That's what I intend to do with this book: give the reader enough of a story to fill a half-hour's worth of reading time and to leave them sitting on the edge of their seats wondering what new horror tomorrow will bring.

On My Poetry

I normally don't title my poetry, but I have decided to do so for the sake of simplicity in putting them in this book. There is something you will notice about the poetry I write. I don't like titles, and I don't like capitalization or punctuation. Certain people may balk at my writing style, but writing "correctly" just doesn't feel right. I feel that I can't portray my feelings the way I want them to be felt if I were to use correct punctuation and capitalization.

I like poetry that tells a story.

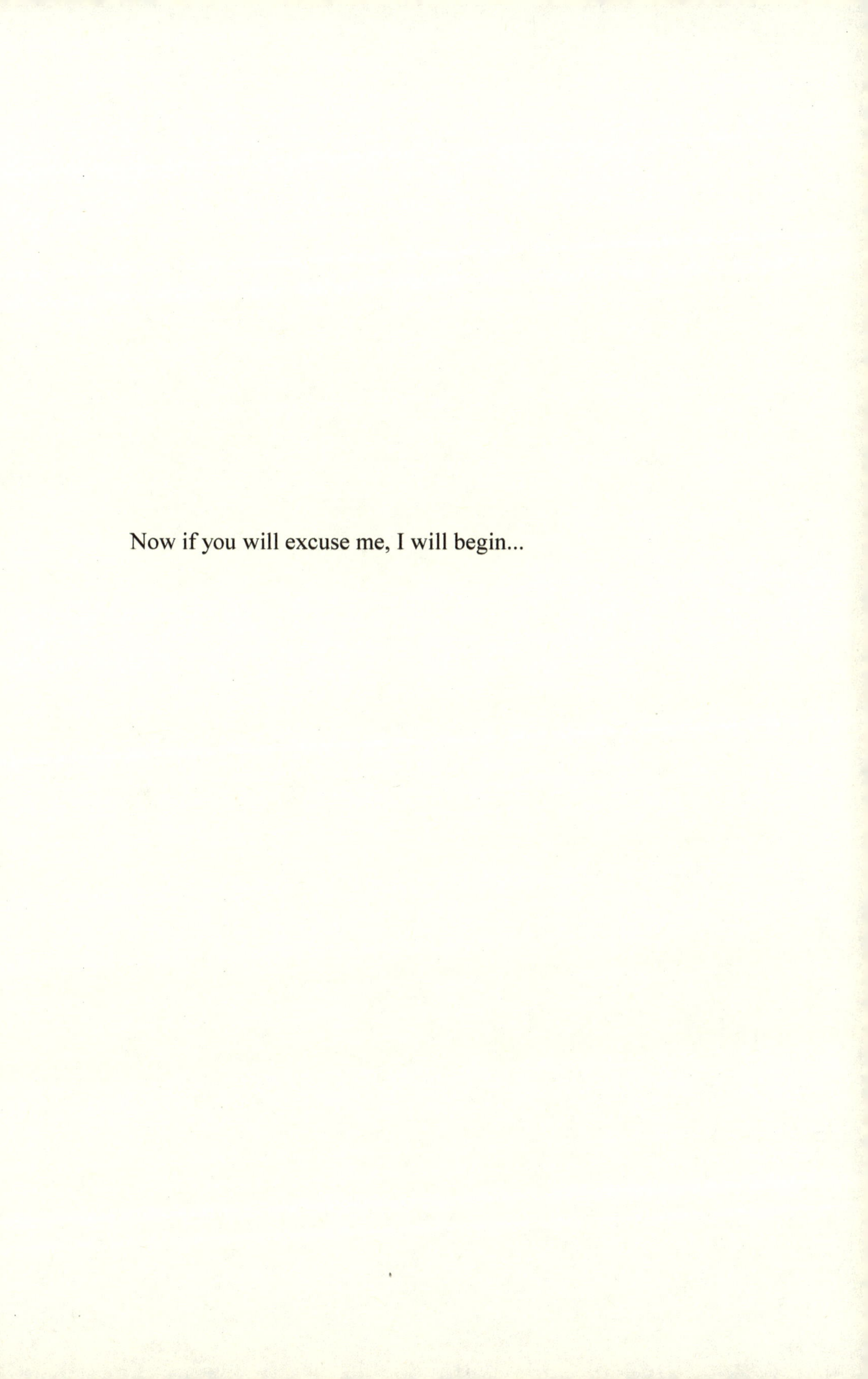

Now if you will excuse me, I will begin...

Day One

The Tale of William Storey

William Storey died in a fright that no man should ever know. On his deathbed he began to see all the people he had murdered during his eighty two years, without the ability to determine if they were just hallucinations brought on by the last four bottles of whiskey he had consumed to help take the pain away or if they were actually in the room. It did not matter to him; all he knew was they were there, and they scared him.

See, old Bill had been shot in the gut by an eight-year-old boy. Earlier that hot summer's day, he had come upon a quaint little farmhouse down in Apache Valley. Racked with hunger from three days in the Great Desert without food, he was desperate. Bill needed food and he was going to get it.

With his equally old revolver hidden between his crotch and the saddle horn, he slowly rode down the narrow path leading to the front of the house. He had inherited his father's two revolvers after he had died; it was his father's wish that they be passed from one generation to the next. Little did he know they would only be handed down once and come to be in the hands of an eight-year-old not in his blood line. As Bill approached the house, a man slowly opened the heavy oak front door and stepped outside.

As the newcomer to our story walked the seven paces from the front door to the hitching posts that constituted a fence, he took stock of the old man on horseback slowly approaching him. He rode hunched over, one hand on the reins, another apparently holding the saddle horn, with his Stetson hanging low as to hide the whole of his face. It was apparent this tired old cowboy needed sustenance and a place to lay his head, and the man was more than willing to provide anything he could for someone who had the wherewithal to brave the Great Desert. He had done so many times before; at least once a year some dumb son of a bitch would show up at his front door sunburned to the bone and thirsty enough to drink an ocean. Death was more often than not at their heels and old William Storey was no exception.

"Howdy!"

"Howdy," replied the old man. It was clear that he had run out of water days ago, his windpipe sore and dry from the lack of it.

"Need a rest, old friend?"

He cocked his head to the side, finally allowing the man a full view of his latest visitor. "Might be nice."

"Conquered the Great, did ya?"

With a quick, almost inaudible chuckle, "Yup, s'pose I did."

"Well get off that horse and take yourself a seat there in the shade by the door. I've got three rocking chairs there, any one of them yours for the takin'. I'll hitch and water your horse for ya."

"Much obliged."

"And after that, I'll go fix up some supper for ya. I've got enough store to feed the whole English Navy."

"Much obliged, much obliged, my boy."

As old Bill dismounted, the man caught a glimpse of the revolver in his hand. "Whatcha keepin' that out for? Ain't nuttin' out there in the Great."

With another small chuckle and a slight smirk: "I know that now."

Both men laughed. Bill could feel the fatigue in his bones; it made him stumble a bit. He hoped the stranger didn't take note of it.

"There's a well 'round back. Why don't you go quench yerself while I finish up here?"

With that, the old man started toward the back of the house, stopping briefly a few times to regain his composure. He didn't want to let his weakness overtake him. If he passed out, he was fair game with this stranger.

At the base of the well was a small rain barrel, a ceramic cup sitting atop its lid. Bill just stood there, unable to decide what course of action to take. If he drank from the barrel, he would surely come down with the Sick in the next couple of hours. He didn't care though; he hadn't had a drink of water for five days and he was too weak to work the pump by himself.

After much deliberation, he opened the barrel and poured several cups full of the cool water over his head. As tempting as it was though, he didn't dare drink any. He knew what would happen; the Sick would overtake and possibly kill him. The water seemed to re-energize him, and using the cup, he primed the pump and began working the handle up and down. It took ten cycles for water to start flowing out of the faucet. Bill looked down - no bucket! He took off his Stetson and held it under the faucet with one hand while he worked the handle again with the other, filling it to the brim with just two pumps. The old cowboy lifted the hat to his lips and gulped the water down as fast as it would pour out.

How sweet it was! Cold and fresh, with a slight hint of saltiness from the sweat stains bordering the rim. Water never tasted so good.

Before he knew it, he had drunk the whole lot. His hat held nearly a gallon and he'd gulped the whole thing in nearly three minutes. Placing the cold wet Stetson back atop his head felt like an ice block, instantly cooling him down and began driving away the headache caused by the glaring sun.

He looked around for the bucket, only to find it twenty yards or so away from the well. The frequent windstorms must have caught it and lifted it off the pump's faucet and carried it away. Luckily its handle had snagged on a small cactus, preventing it from being lost forever in the Great. With renewed energy, he filled the bucket and dumped its entire contents over his body, washing away the weeks of sand that plastered his body.

"Don't see old, wet cowboys 'round here that much!" the other man exclaimed with a smile.

"Don't s'pose you do." said old Bill. Looking down at the ground at the spot where the first splashes of water had landed, he came to know how hot it really was. It appeared dry as a bone already.

"How 'bout that supper?"

"You got it, old friend."

2

As old Bill traveled the West, he made many an enemy of the people unfortunate enough to cross his path and live to tell about it. Even his equally old stallion Saguaro hated him, but remained loyal and trustworthy because of the fact that old Bill was all he knew.

He had never broken bread with a man such as John Riley. In fact, it was a rare occasion when he *did* break bread in the company of another man. He did not like company.

John was unlike anyone he had met before; John befriended him without question. He had an aura of love around him, the kind of love you could feel emanating from his very body. It was as if an invisible comforting hand reached out and laid itself on your shoulder whenever his attention was on you.

Bill had never had a real friend before and found himself wondering what it was like to live in such a way as John did. Even as a child, young William had always shied away from other boys and girls his age; he never went to school. He knew nothing but thievery. His father had taught him the ways of the cowboy at the tender age of six and taught him the way of the gun shortly thereafter. He was a sharpshooter at age twelve, unmatched by even the most skilled of the most skilled. There was no top tier for Bill. Hell, he *was* the top tier. His guns were his friends.

"Cornbread's good." he said, a small rivulet of oil leaving his lip, making its way toward the thickening mass of hairs on his chin. His beard was well along. He hadn't shaved in at least two weeks before he even came to the Great.

"Thanks, old friend. That's my mama's recipe." He stopped for a second, debating whether or not to divulge Mama's secret.

Oh what the hell, she's dead anyway!

"Peppers and un-yuns, an' a little bit of cheese."

"Well it's damn good. Yer mama was a right genius."

"I say thankya again! And so does Mama!"

"Say, why ya keep callin' me old friend?"

"I dunno, s'pose it's 'cause I don't know yer name."

After a moment of silence, the old cowboy wiped his hand clean with the little white cloth that John had given him with dinner. It felt strange using an actual napkin to wipe his hands clean rather than just using his jeans as was the usual case. His hands and lips hadn't seen the use of a napkin in many a long year. It made him feel good inside, as if he was something more than just a thieving cowboy.

As he extended his tan, wrinkled hand, "Name's William, William Storey. Bill if you will."

"Well William Storey...Bill if you will...name's John, John Riley."

Both men shook hands, raised their respective bottles of whiskey, and with a hearty "Cheers!" toasted one another and their newfound friendship. During the next hour they shared the meal of cornbread and beef stew that John had prepared and shared stories of life on the range. It had been so long since old Bill had felt so full he couldn't remember the last time he had been treated to such a feast.

Something was different about this place. Something was different about John. Bill felt wanted here, and that made him feel uneasily comfortable. He had no qualms about letting down his guard around John and even went so far as to take his belt off and leave it hanging on the rocking chair next to him, something he never did unless he found himself alone. He always had his guns within arm's reach, but not here.

"My boy's due back in the mornin'.

"Oh yeah? You got a boy?"

"Yep, eight years old. Sent him into town this mornin' for flour and cornmeal."

"Huh, ain't never heard of no eight-year-old could handle that kinda job before."

"He's a special one. Runs this whole ranch damn near hisself. All I get to do is the cookin' and heavy liftin'. He don't let me do a damn thing, hon'ry little shit he is."

"Learn 'im to shoot yet?"

"Oh yeah, he's quite the shot. Gotta hold the pistol with both hands, but he's still pretty good. See that post there?" John pointed to one of the four hitching posts that lined his yard. Bill hadn't seen the far one. It was full of holes on the side facing the house and looked as if a woodpecker had hit a goldmine and pecked the hell out of it. "That's his doin' right there. He plinks that thing from all the way over here. Rarely misses."

All of a sudden Bill felt a little fright run through his bones. He had been such a shot at the age of eight as well.

"Looks like a .45."

"Yep."

A .45 seemed much too strong for a boy. Hell, even a .22 should be hard enough for an eight-year-old to handle. He imagined the boy firing the gun with the barrel kicking back and slapping him in the face. He managed a sly grin and a muffled chuckle, but that little fright grew to a slight quiver.

3

John had given Bill young Jack's bed for the night. It had been months since he'd slept in an actual bed. He awoke to the smell of fresh coffee boiling on the open fire in the fireplace. John already had an iron skillet heating up and a pound of potatoes cut up and ready to fry.

"Mornin' cowboy!"

"Mornin'."

"Sleep good?"

"Like a baby, I did! Ain't slept like that in ages." In fact, the crick in his back was gone and Bill felt like he could run back across the Great on his own two legs before the day was done.

"Good, good. Ya hungry?"

Old Bill just nodded his head. "Still kinda full from sup, but I think I can give it another go!"

As they sat across the table from one another eating their breakfast of biscuits and fried potatoes, they shared even more stories like two old friends with years to catch up on. Bill never had a friend he could sit down and shoot the shit with over a hearty meal.

They laughed, they ate, and they laughed some more.

When they were done, Bill asked John, "Think ya could do me a favor?"

"What's that?" he asked with a cocked eyelid.

"Ya got any gun oil?"

With that, Bill went to cleaning the revolvers. It wasn't hard to accomplish; they hadn't been used in nearly a month. Save a little dust in the barrel, there really wasn't much to it. After a good oiling on the actions and triggers, they were ready to go.

"What's the story with those, Mister Storey? They look old."

With his usual small smirk, he replied "My pa's."

"Well they's nice. Some fine workmanship there."

"Thankya. Pa had 'em made down in Old Mexico, long 'fore I was born. They's well over a hundred."

As old Bill finished loading up the cylinder on the second of the two guns, he spun it and snapped it closed with a flip of his wrist and laid it on the table in front of him next to the first one. Both barrels were pointed at John, but both men knew there was no danger in it.

John stared in awe of those hundred-year-old guns.

"John, I want to thank you for your hospitality."

"Ah, think nothin' of it."

"Well I owe ya, John. And I think I need to tell ya somethin'."

"What's that?"

"Well John, I'm not a good man. Ain't never been one. Ain't never had a home, either. I ain't never loved a woman; had my fair share of whores, but I ain't never loved. I'm a liar and a thief. I've robbed banks and stagecoaches. That ain't what I wanted to tell you though. John, I..."

"Go on, Bill." John said as he took another long sip of coffee.

"I... I'm a killer. I don't know why I'm telling you this, but I feel I have to. I owe you that. No one has ever treated me the way you have and I feel like I owe it to you. You're the closest thing to a friend that I've ever had."

"I know."

"What?"

"I seen a poster of you in town last week. Five hundred dollars they're giving for you."

Bill dropped his coffee cup and grabbed a revolver, pointing it at John's head, cocked and ready with his ass off the chair before the cup even hit the tabletop. It bounced on its side, sending hot coffee across the table, all over John. Bill was damn fast for a man of eighty-plus years.

Without so much as a flinch, John said, "Put that down, Bill. You don't need it."

"And why's that?"

"I ain't turnin' you in, now put that down."

"Why you so calm? You serious?"

"Dead. Now I wanna tell *you* somethin', Bill."

Bill sat back down, still pointing the pistol at John. John wiped the coffee from his shirt and face, cleared his throat, and began. "I ain't who ya think I am either, old friend. My boy don't know this, and I pray he don't ever, but I'm you. Well, used to be you; I'm retired."

"Do tell?"

"I robbed my last bank before my wife came up pregnant nine years ago. She died when Jack was born. I settled this here spread when my dear old Sarah told me about the baby. We never had a home before this place, much like you. On this side of the Great, no one knew who I was, so this is where we set root." They had wanted an honest life for their son, and the only way to do it was cross the Great so they could take new names and start over.

"She died in the very bed you slept in last night, Jack's bed."

"Why are you telling me this?"

The hand holding the revolver began to shake. He didn't notice the little tin coffee cup sitting on the edge of the table. His shaking gradually moved it farther and farther over the edge until it finally became unbalanced and fell to the floor. When it hit the floor, the metallic clang startled Bill, and before John knew it, a .45 slug whizzed past his head and lodged itself in a log in the wall behind him.

Neither of them heard the second shot. Their ears were still deafened from the first. Bill fell sideways onto the floor, the chair falling over with him.

"Bill!" John sprang up and quickly knelt down beside the old cowboy, trying to make sense of what had just happened. Out of the corner of his eye, he saw a small black silhouette standing in the open doorway. Young Jack had come home early.

"He *is* good. Got me right in the gut," Bill said as he looked up at John and smiled. "Taught him good, you did."

Young Jack never moved. He stood in the doorway with the Winchester carbine pointed straight at old Bill at the ready. "Jack, get over here! Help me!"

"Daddy, I..."

"Never mind that, help me!"

They lifted Bill and carried him back to Jack's bed.

4

John and little Jack both sat at Bill's side until nightfall. They did everything they could to stop the bleeding, but it was no use. He had lost so much blood he drifted unwillingly in and out of consciousness as the day crept on.

Finally gaining control over his wrinkled, fluttering eyelids, - it had taken him the better part of an hour to concentrate his efforts - he spoke. "John, go east to Georgia. Should be three months' ride. When you get to Atlanta, ride northeast for three days and look for Snodon. It's a little town, ain't much there. Ask someone to point you to the

Nodoroc."

"The Nodoroc?"

"Yeah, Nodoroc. It's a big lake of boiling mud, ain't never seen anything like it, but the Indians think it's the gateway to Hell. Stinks like nothin' you ever smelled too. There's a big plume of smoke coming from it. You'll be able to see it for miles, almost like a house is on fire in the distance."

"What's there?"

Bill's eyes closed. John shook him gently. "Bill, what's there?"

"John, there's people behind you." John looked around the room, startled. No one was there but Jack.

Death's got a hold of him. Won't be long now.

"Are there?" After a little pause, "What's at the Nodoroc, Bill?"

"My money. A hair over fifty thousand dollars I buried there. Look for an old oak tree with a large boulder at its base. It's within ten paces of the boulder. Mind the mud. If you step in it, you're as good as gone." Bill looked around the room again. "John, who are all these people?"

"Bill, no one's here 'cept me and Jack. Why do ya want me to have that money?"

"Yer the closest thing I ever had to a friend, John Riley."

As Bill looked at the figures around the room, their previously blacked-out faces began to change hue, and color began to fill them. He stared in amazement as one by one they became clearer and clearer. Eventually he started to recognize them; they were the people he had murdered throughout the years.

The old Mexican was there; he'd killed him just last week and took his coin sack; Silas Conley, the farrier who charged him too much for new shoes last year; Mae Smith, the whore in Tennessee who didn't want to provide *all* services paid for; his cousin Brian, who'd cheated him in an innocent game of cards, who he bludgeoned to death with a log from the fireplace. More and more people walked into the room as the minutes ticked by.

As John fed him his fourth bottle of whiskey, he became increasingly frightened. The people inched closer and closer to him and he couldn't get away. Paralysis quickly took hold of his body, not by physical cause but by pure and unadulterated fear.

"John..."

"Yeah Bill?" His hand gripped the old man's hand even tighter.

"They're here."

"What Bill...William?"

"For me..."

When they began to lay their cold hands on Bill, he could feel the life being sucked out of him. Even though their faces had gained color, their eyes had remained black and seemed to grow blacker by the second. And their teeth, oh God, their teeth! Each one of their mouths was filled with double rows of sharp pointed yellowed teeth.

He opened his mouth to speak; he wanted so badly to tell John what was happening, but he couldn't, for it was his ability to speak that was the first thing to go. It looked like all seventy six people were now crammed into the room. How, he could not figure. But they were there.

Closer and closer they came. His cousin's hands had fingers with nails like knives. He sank them deep into Bill's leg, ripped out a small chunk, and brought it to his mouth. The pain was unbearable. The only sound he could hear was the smacking of his cousin's wet lips, like a coyote lapping up the blood of a freshly felled goat.

Each time the apparition plunged its hand into Bill's leg, he pulled out another small chunk and handed it to the figure behind him. They would eat and then pass the next piece back to whoever was behind them. After nearly passing out from the pain – his aged heart could hardly take it – Bill looked down to find his thigh ripped down to the bone.

"It's time, William." Brian said with a voice so deep and sickening that it made him throw up. In one swift move, his cousin's hand plunged deep into his stomach, up under his rib cage, wrapped itself around his heart and began to squeeze.

He began convulsing, and his eyes widened. John held tightly to old Bill's hand, trying to assure him that everything was okay. His body shook violently, unlike any death he had ever seen from a mere gunshot. The only time he had ever witnessed such a thing was the time he poisoned the butcher. The bastard was known for cheating people. He had been caught on numerous occasions weighting his scales so he could charge people more money for less meat.

Young Jack grabbed Bill's other hand and held it tightly as well. He was scared. He had never taken a life before. Everything he had ever killed before was out of necessity; the errant coyote after the chicken coop, a pig here and there, a couple of cows, and of course the usual hen every week for supper. He had never taken a *human* life before.

After all, he *was* just a boy.

What have I done?

The old cowboy's eyes rolled into the back of his head and his world turned black.

Day Two

Wolves

my body is weary
my mind in a fog
i hear the barking
of a faraway dog

i open the door
with rifle in tow
and step with bare feet
into the cold wet snow

yet i do not notice
because from all around
comes the incessant barking
of an aged red hound

i cannot find the direction
from which it is coming
and i do not even notice
how quickly my feet are numbing

i trek across my land
looking for the tracks
that will lead me to this beast
when i notice the pain in my back

and suddenly i come to know
i cannot feel my feet
but to rid myself of this monster
would bring me a sense of peace

i can no longer feel pain
in these tired old feet of mine
it has long since left my calves
and started its trek up my spine

i look back towards home
only to see a different scene
and gone is the path
that led to where i have been

as i turned back around
i found myself in a field
a desert with dogs all around
with no space to yield

the snow had grown deeper
the barking had ceased
i now stood eye to eye
with a hundred growling beasts

i shouldered my rifle
and took aim at the first
and realized i had only one shot
the feeling was the worst

the dogs had turned to wolves
ready to attack
suddenly i felt a new pain
shooting up my back

one had lunged
and bitten me
from my blind side
from whence i could not see

backwards i fell
into the snow
i had no chance
nowhere to go

they tore at my legs
yet i could not feel
and from the corner of my eye
i saw a flash of steel

in my fall i dropped my rifle
the muzzle landing at my head
and the butt was sitting by my hip
in my cold and bloody bed

two more grabbed my arms
and started tearing fiercely
i was not defenseless
yet feeling pain so scarcely

i thanked the snow
for numbing my limbs
and hoped that quickly
this nightmare would end

i tilted my head downward
just in time to see a paw
slip into the trigger guard
and that was the end of it all

i awoke in a cold sweat
sitting upright in my bed
trying to shake the confusion
as well as the feeling of dread

then i heard the barking
of that damned old red hound
and before i even knew it
running i hit the ground

through the door
with rifle in tow
i ran outside
into the cold wet snow

i flung myself around
to face the place where i had been
and then i came to realize
my nightmare was about to begin

Day Three

Set in Stone

"January second, two thousand and nine, six thirty-two P.M., Ronald McClaine interview," the aged interrogator said as he set the digital recorder down on the tabletop. The years had taken their toll on him, rewarding him with deep crow's feet and a bad back that required the majority of his days in a chair, which in turn gave him quite the gut. A bacon, egg, and cheese biscuit, a double order of hash browns, and a large coffee were his daily morning fare for the past eleven years, and it showed.

He started in law enforcement in 1972 at the tender age of twenty as a beat cop in Detroit. His father was a cop, and his father before that. It was only right that he become a cop; just hoping like hell that he wouldn't die on the job and follow in their footsteps to *that* extent. A bullet through the side of the abdomen in 1980 courtesy of a strung-out crackhead with a hatred for pigs – a bad combination – put an end to his beat days, and he retired to the desk, fulfilling a half-assed dream of becoming a detective.

His father was a detective toward the end of his career, something his old man had longed for since childhood. It was his father's dream, not his. Back in the summer of '76, Papa was scouring a murder scene in a run-down row house collecting evidence and came across an easy chair with a bomb hidden beneath the seat cushion.

The detective's fifty-seven years looked like seventy-five to the casual passer-by.

Ronald McClaine sat across the nondescript white table from him, hands bound by a pair of shiny stainless steel handcuffs. Two armed guards stood on either side of the only door into the little cinderblock room. It was a dull gray steel door, slightly darker than the gray paint covering the walls, accented by a single thin-paned window impregnated with wire mesh above the handle on the right side. Scuff marks and small dents covered the bottom half where people had kicked it in violent protest of their incarceration.

A big cobweb in one corner gently swayed in a breeze that no one could feel, presumably from a small crack in the mortar allowing air to leak in from the hallway outside. And the smell; there was mold somewhere in those walls. One wouldn't be surprised to find rats scurrying in those walls either. That is, assuming they could navigate their way through the holes in the blocks.

Dank, dark, smelly. This room was meant to depress, its sole purpose to break a man. A day alone in this room could easily drive a man to madness. Or make him sick – quite possibly both.

2

"Mister McClaine, please tell me about how you murdered Sally Trent."

With nary a glimpse of emotion, Ronald replied, "I hit her in the head." His response mirrored that of a small child matter-of-factly stating the obvious in that naive fashion in which children so often do. McClaine came across as more of a child than the middle-aged man he appeared to be.

"We gathered that, Mister McClaine."

"Call me Ron."

"Mister McClaine, please tell me, in detail..."

"I said call me Ron, or I won't cooperate anymore." Ron wanted the power, whatever the situation. Even in his school-boy days he longed for it, but never achieved it. Little Ronnie was always the short fat kid with the asthma problem, the one the other kids bullied and made fun of. That is, until the day he beat Billy Younger to a bloody pulp on the baseball field with an aluminum bat for hitting him with a pitch one too many times.

Billy Younger learned his lesson. He never walked again.

That was in eighth grade. The courts couldn't try him as an adult and sent him away to a juvenile detention facility to live out the remainder of his days until he reached adulthood.

They assumed he was rehabilitated when they released him five years later. They assumed. *What happens when you assume, Ronnie? You makes an ass outta* you *and* me*! They's a buncha asses in there. They's dum asses, sho 'nuff!*

Little Ronnie inherited a copy of *How to Win Friends and Influence People* from the poor son of a bitch who'd lived in his room before him. In fact, the sucker had left a whole bookshelf in there filled with self-help books, and the orderlies were apparently too lazy to take it out of there and file the books in the library as ordered.

Sometimes Ronnie found himself wondering about the previous tenant. Part of him hoped that whoever it was had truly rehabilitated himself enough to get out there in the world and be productive and have a good life. The other part of him knew what was perhaps more likely, that the kid had hanged himself in the shower room believing that he would finally be set free. Sometimes kids did that, the ones with the *really* long sentences.

At any rate, Ronnie learned a lot from that Dale Carnegie. Dale was a damn smart man. That book became his lifeblood. Ronnie read it from cover to cover once a month for four and a half years and could recite any chapter word for word if you asked him to.

That book made him quite the businessman. He studied concrete construction religiously during his tenure, and upon his release moved to Florida and opened a cast-stone manufacturing plant of his own – not too shabby for an eighteen-year-old greenhorn. He was always intrigued by the limestone architectural accents on the skyscrapers in the books from the library.

Ron became quite successful in his venture, in short time growing to be one of the country's foremost authorities on cast stone, further refining the process and inventing new ways to manufacture it. He patented a fiberglass mesh reinforcing system that completely replaced the rebar inserts most commonly found in the stone. This being the case, many construction companies had turned to him in search of a better, stronger product, making him a self-made millionaire in just a few short years. He was a prodigy in the industry.

He bought a home on the Gulf Coast at only twenty-one and an old but seaworthy wooden vessel shortly thereafter, and opened a somewhat lucrative side business providing deep-sea fishing tours on Saturdays and Sundays.

3

Frustrated, the interrogator tried again. "Okay Ron, please tell me, in detail, how did you kill Miss Trent?"

Sally Trent had been loading boxes of personal belongings into the back of her hatchback when Ronald happened to catch a glimpse of her out of the corner of his eye as he drove by. Her two Chihuahuas had ruined the carpet in her apartment with nearly a year of piss stains, even managing to pull it up and chew it to shreds in the corners just to complete the destruction. Recently receiving an amended schedule at the diner, she could ill afford the eight-hundred-plus-dollar replacement cost. The economy just wasn't good, and the flow of customers had ebbed considerably. Save the handful of regulars, the vast majority of seats remained empty from day to day.

The landlord had stopped by for his annual inspection just the day before and was not at all pleased with what he saw. The very morning Sally was murdered, her landlord had slipped an envelope under her door with a letter explaining that she was to move out by the end of the week and that even worse, she had forfeited her rather substantial security deposit, which she was counting on. Without it, she had to borrow money from her mother to pay for the deposit on the next apartment she found, something she was not proud of doing. Sally almost hated the bitch. If it weren't for the fact that she was her mother, Sally's disdain would have crossed the line to all-out hatred years ago.

Seeing an opportunity to right some of the wrongs he had done in his life, Ron found a spot to park and walked down the alley to see if the young brunette could use some help. Who knows, maybe he could help her. Maybe he could offer to buy her a drink at the bar he spotted around the corner, maybe even dinner. Maybe he could flash a little money and get lucky.

The sun was quickly setting and the alley growing dim. She had only three boxes left to load up and take to the storage unit she had rented at noon.

"Need some help, ma'am?"

"Oh God, yes. Thank you so much!"

Smiling, he replied "Not a problem ma'am. Always willing to help a damsel in distress."

She smiled back and said in her best feigned Southern accent, "Why thank ya, kind sir!"

Sally loaded the final box, but it wouldn't quite fit. "Could you?" she asked, slightly embarrassed. As she stepped back, he reached past her, his right arm "accidentally" brushing her left breast. While the gesture held no meaning for her, it was a well-calculated and well-executed move on his part.

The quick glimpse of fantasy flashed through his mind. He imagined himself grabbing her tit with his left hand and a wad of hundreds in his right. In the next instant she was on her knees pulling down his zipper.

Removing two cast iron skillets from the box behind it allowed him to bend the side of the box in slightly so the other one would fit. Holding one in each hand, he turned around and said, "There's your problem, little lady."

"Oh, my knight in shining armor!"

They smiled at each other. The alley had become dark, save for a lone street light in the distance.

"Just carry these in your front seat and you'll be fine."

"Here, let me get the door for you."

As they walked around the passenger side of the car, that feeling came over him again. It was now dark, he was in his element. Although he had tried in earnest to do good today, the demon in him came forward and took over. His eyes ran down her back.

What a nice piece of ass!

Her shapely backside squeezed into the tight, low-cut jeans she was wearing created that well-defined line where ass cheek meets upper thigh, barely moving as her hips swayed from side to side. He even caught a glimpse of dim light shining through that part of the crotch where the combination of tight jeans and well toned thighs creates that little upside-down triangle. This was the clincher. This is what the demon liked.

Oh, what he wouldn't have given to fuck her. He lived for the girls half his age; they moved like no other.

It only took one swing to end her life. She was only five foot two and a smidgen over a buck-ten, after all. She couldn't have bested the most average man. Before Ron could rein in the demon, he raised his right hand, holding the heaviest of the two iron skillets, and brought it crashing down on the back of her head with a dull thud. The force of the blow split the back of her skull open and simultaneously slid the top vertebra to the side just enough to sever her spinal cord.

It happened so fast she never felt the first twinge of pain.

And that was good.

4

"...and that's when you caught me."

The nosy neighbor across the alley had called the police. He had been spying on Sally from his bedroom window with a pair of night vision binoculars, as he did every night. She always came home from work late. He longed for her. *She's out of your league, buddy!*

As soon as she hit the ground, the young man sprang into action and ran through his apartment and dialed 911. Luckily, two cops were just around the corner at the very bar that Ron had planned to take Sally so he could get her liquored up. They ran into the alley and caught him before he could finish stuffing her body into the passenger seat of her car.

He had *planned* on dropping her car over on 57th, downtown, where all the crack heads were known to hang out and the deals went down. Her body he would take to *the plant.*

The interrogator stared at McClaine, dumbfounded.

At once, the interrogator leapt from his chair, hurling himself across the table, and wrapped his hands around McClaine's throat. The two guardsmen smiled.

"Anything else you want to tell me?" he asked, with an obvious lump in his throat.

"Well I'm done for, so I figure I might as well. I've been waiting for you people to catch up to me, although I *did* hope it would have been the FBI and not some pissant city cops."

When McClain had the plant built, he had the offices built – his office, namely – with a secret door hidden in a bookshelf, opening to a stairway that led down into a secret room. On the plans it read

EMERGENCY STORM SHELTER

and that was its original intent, at least it *had* been.

But his turnover rate had been so high over the course of the years that there was no one left of his original crew; therefore, no one to know of the shelter.

Or the tub in it.

Five gallon buckets sat beneath the stairs with *CHUM* haphazardly written across them in black permanent marker. Along one wall, a makeshift cinder block and plywood workbench with a meat grinder bolted to it. Next to it, a hydraulic shop press with a fine dusting of white powder on the floor below it, haphazardly speckled with small chunks resembling the tiny remains of well-used chalk sticks.

In the end, Ron confessed to sixty-three murders around the coastal area. The majority of them had been lonely teenage girls he'd picked up toward the end of spring break after the crowds had died down. He usually found them jogging along the back road, away from the more congested frontal road that overlooked the ocean. He always targeted the ones wearing the spandex biker shorts.

The back road was normally quiet, the kind of place where you could easily flash a girl a couple of hundreds and get her into your car without being spotted.

The younger they were, the easier they were to get.

5

I can't believe it! We finally caught the sonofabitch!

Whenever a missing persons case came across his desk, the interrogator just knew the same guy was responsible. Something deep in his detective's gut told him so, and if it told him so, it was right. It was always the same: young girl, out for a jog, last seen wearing tight-fitting clothing. And they were always quite the lookers.

The interrogator rose from the table, trying his damnedest to hide the trembling in his hands. “Guards, I need a break.”

6

“Mister McClaine, explain something to me. You claim to have murdered...sixty-three?”

“Yes.”

“...sixty-three people. Pray tell, where are the bodies?”

“The Deep.”

“*Where's* that?” he asked with a hint of confusion.

"The Deep…the ocean. The *Gulf of Mexico*."

He told the interrogator about the room beneath his office. A patrol car was immediately dispatched to the plant with the combination to the lock embedded in the paneling behind the stone finial he used for a bookend. *It swings shut by itself. You can get back out, but you need the combination to get back in.*

"How so? Care to tell me?"

"My charters. The chum." *That's how you bait sharks, you clueless shit head! Do you know your ass from a hole in the ground?*

A stab of rage shot through the detective's body. **"You chum the water with... *people?*"**

"Sure do!" McClaine exclaimed matter-of-factly. "Why do you think I've been so successful?"

Truth be told, it was the only way he could rid himself of evidence of his crimes. It was the reason he started the charter in the first place.

"I don't chum the bones though." *People would see them. They'd ask questions. And I don't chum the meat either, just the blood and the useless shit.*

With heartburn setting in, fighting off the urge to vomit all over the table, the detective gathered himself as best he could. "What do you do with the bones, Ron?"

7

There was always a plastic container marked

One Cup Per Cube
Ronnie's Special Ingredient

sitting on the shelf next to the cement mixer in the same bold permanent marker that marked the chum buckets. The linesman working the mixer only questioned it once to find its secrecy so well protected that Colonel Sanders had *nothing* on it.

That fine white powder had been used in batch after batch, year after year, job after job. Stone after stone.

The interrogator sat across from McClaine with the same

dumbfounded look on his face as before.

"I crush 'em up. Add it to the mix. Makes it easy to get rid of."

"How many..."

"Stones, I presume? Hundreds...thousands...tens of thousands, I suppose."

Dumbfounded.

"Look, go to the county. Get a list of all projects built since 1996. Every building 'round here with cast stone on it has bone in it. Test it. You'll see I'm telling the truth. I have no reason to lie now."

What about the meat grinder?

"Chum and stone. Is that all, Ron? Something tells me you're not telling me everything."

Hmmmph. "No, I'm not."

"On with it," the interrogator demanded, like a schoolteacher trying to coax a child into confession, motioning his right hand in a circular fashion in the air in front of him.

Ronald debated spilling the beans. Why the hell not? He'd gone this far.

"I eat them, too."

Both guards grimaced. One trained his right hand on the butt of his revolver. The interrogator jumped up and ran to the garbage can, emptying himself of his breakfast along the way.

Meat is meat. Don't taste no diff'rent from anything else! Ron had no qualms about it and had never understood the taboo. If people would only try it instead of bastardizing it, they would see what they were missing. The thought of a sixteen-year-old girl's rack of ribs smoking on the grill sent his taste buds into a frenzy, making his mouth water with excitement.

8

He stared at Ron through the wired window in the door for a few minutes. *There* is no *composing myself after that.*

9

When he re-entered the room he tread lightly, as to avoid the splattering of the pink, slimy stomach goo he had spilled onto the floor. “Guards, a minute alone please?”

When they stepped out, he rushed over and threw the dead bolt. It was just he and McClaine now. And McClaine was in hand and ankle cuffs with a chain connecting the two.

Both guards immediately began pounding on the door when they heard the click, demanding to re-enter. It was all in vain; he wasn't listening and the door was soundproof.

A split second later, he had crossed the room and shoved the table against McClaine, pinning him to the wall. Fists flew into the murderer’s face as he sat there, unable to free himself. The onslaught was more than he could handle. *This old man's sure sure got some steam left in 'im.*

The room faded out.

10

When he regained consciousness, the table had been pushed aside and the old interrogator was sitting in a chair in front of him. “Been waiting for you to come to, Mister McClaine.”

Ron's eyes were already swelling from his beating, and he could barely make out what the interrogator was holding in his hand. The muffled cries and pounding continued to pour in from outside, meeting their ears as nothing more than low, unintelligible mumbles.

When he squinted, he could make out the shape of a cigar cutter. “Good time for a smoke, huh?” he asked with a slight smirk, further conveying his you-can-just-kiss-my-ass mentality to him.

“Oh, this ain't for the stogie.” the interrogator said, his eyes beginning to well with tears.

Just a stogie? What, ain't rich enough to buy a real *cigar, asshole?*

The worn-down interrogator took McClaine's right hand with

his left and slid the cutter over his index finger. McClaine's eyes widened, and he gasped as the horror of his fate became clear. His chest began to heave as his heart beat tripled and threatened to tear it's way through his rib cage. He bucked and kicked with all his might, but it was useless – he had been restrained, tied to the chair if you will, to the chair with cuttings from his own shirt.

"Sally Trent was my niece, you piece o' shit."

Day Four

Jeremy Willard and the Old Gray Squirrel

The old gray squirrel perched precariously atop the highest branch of the old Scrub Oak, watching what was left of its brood feeding from the little house-shaped bird feeder that hung from the shepherd's hook in Jeremy Willard's backyard. Her offspring was as carefree and fast as she was in her days of youth, and she lived vicariously through him. Not by choice, mind you; she was up in age and not as nimble as those half her age. Deep inside she longed for those days to come 'round again. She missed the dexterity that once allowed her to sprint along fence tops and along power lines. She missed the speed and agility that once allowed her to escape the occasional diving hawk or striking snake. Those days had come and gone, and she was relegated to spending her days sitting in her nest high in that old Scrub Oak, waiting for the last of her young to bring her sunflower seeds that the robins and finches refused to eat.

This little guy was the last; the last of her last litter. She birthed three this time around. Her body just couldn't handle another litter. Of the three, one had fallen out of the nest just days after being born, meeting death when he hit an exposed root at the foot of the tree. Another had been plucked from a lower branch far below in the early-morning mist a few months back by none other than the barn owl that frequented the area in search of prey. Yes, this was the only one left.

She stared adoringly down at him, watching him forage, when all of a sudden a loud "THWAP!" echoed across the peaceful landscape. Simultaneously, her youngest performed a double somersault from the bird feeder and landed on the ground, motionless. From the corner of her eye she caught the sunlight briefly reflecting off of the blued, cold steel barrel of Jeremy's newest pellet rifle as it retreated through the window facing the feeder. She had lost herself in the moment and never noticed the silent and slow movement of the window opening.

Jeremy had a new trick up his sleeve; a new trick with a new gun. He had mounted the scope on a pair of see-through rings to give it enough height to be able to stick the barrel through the opening created by the barely opened window and still be able to see over a two-inch-tall piece of wood that made the bottom of the window. The squirrels had become accustomed to the sound of the back door opening, and they would retreat as soon as they heard it, for Jeremy would more likely than not have one of his death sticks in tow. This new tactic was perfect.

Anger, no, rage coursed through her body when she finally registered what had just happened. Adrenaline shot through her veins and the strength of a locomotive filled her frail old body. Her eyes darting back and forth from the body of her youngest son to the window, she began rocking to and fro, fighting the urge to run down the tree and rescue him. It was her better judgment that kept her there, for she knew that if she attempted a rescue, she would surely meet the same fate.

When she finally calmed down to the point she could once again think rationally, the sun had set. Since her son had met his death, she could think of only one thing. Her life was consumed with it to the point of madness. Jeremy Willard had to die.

That night she risked her own death at the hand of the barn owl and quietly made her way down the tree and across the lawn to the house. As she passed the shepherd's hook, she took notice of the place where her son's body once lay; he had been carried off by the neighbor's calico hours before, a sight that sent her further into the depths of madness. She found a spot beneath the deck and began chewing.

She chewed with abandon. Within ten minutes she broke through the wood siding. Within fifteen, a hole big enough to fit through. After another five, she had chewed through the drywall and found herself in the kitchen of the little blue ranch house that Jeremy called home.

All that chewing had effectively drained the life out of her. Tired and covered with gypsum from head to toe, she crawled into the living room and tucked herself under the sofa to avoid detection should Jeremy awaken and discover her handiwork. She needed a rest, and she needed it badly. Her marathon had thus far completely depleted her tired old body. She needed sustenance if she was to have enough energy to carry out her assassination.

Lying there, she could smell the succulent aroma of oranges. Age had not yet killed her sense of smell. Her nose told her where she could find the orange ball of life; on top of the coffee table merely a foot above where she lay.

After a much deserved rest, she crawled out from under the sofa and with renewed energy leapt onto the table above. Before her sat a hand-turned rosewood bowl with not one but five big, plump, ripe Valencias, all for her taking. She sank her teeth into the one nearest her and chewed again for all she was worth. She had eaten an orange only one other time in her life, back when the old people lived there, back before Jeremy came along and ruined everything.

The old people were nice people. Back in those days the backyard was safe, a haven for birds and squirrels alike. The old people would spread all sorts of goodness across the lush green lawn: bread, bits of fruits and vegetables, and nuts, seeds, and berries from a seemingly bottomless white bucket. She didn't know what came of the old people. One day a big white van with flashing lights took them away and things changed.

The combination of her longing for days of old and the citrus filling her tiny stomach triggered a new burst of adrenaline and sent her sprinting down the hallway in search of the snoring that she just knew was Jeremy Willard. Sure enough, her assumption proved right. As she rounded the corner and entered the bedroom, she abruptly stopped and looked up to see his right arm dangling slightly from the edge of the bed.

She jumped up onto the table at the foot of his bed, then up onto the bed itself. For nearly half an hour she just sat there, staring at her sleeping tormentor...now her victim. She slowly and stealthily made her way around the body lying before her, up and down his side, then back and forth across his feet, taking stock of what she had to work with. Where were humans vulnerable? The answer seemed to be too elusive and her patience was growing thin.

Suddenly it revealed itself. He slept with his head back and his neck exposed. In the dim light of the moon creeping in through the window, she could make out the throbbing of the carotid artery, as if it were begging, saying, “Here I am! Bite me!” She inched closer and closer, trying with all her might not to make the slightest sound or motion that would stir him.

After pausing for a moment to gather herself and regain her composure, she sank her teeth in deep and hard and began her third round of vicious chewing for the night. Her first two rounds were child's play to what she was doing now. If he didn't wake up and kill her, the toll the night's activities were exacting on her body surely would. She didn't care. The last of her last was all she had left to live for, and he was gone.

Jeremy awoke with a jolt that very well could have rocked the whole world. Instinctively, his hands began swatting away at the thing that was biting him, but it refused to budge. A moment later, he grasped hold of it and tore it from his neck and hurled it across the room into the wall.

The impact instantly broke her back and she fell to the floor with a squeal that only a small animal in immense pain can make. Jeremy recognized the sound; it was the sound the birds used to make when he shot them with the B.B. gun as a kid. He would maim them, then use a utility knife to cut their wings off before beheading them.

He cupped his neck with his left hand, but it was all in vain. When he ripped her from his own body, she was mid-bite and in turn ripped a large chunk of artery out with her. He could feel his heart pumping with excitement and the hot blood flowing through his fingers despite his best effort to prevent it from escaping.

He arose and felt the life draining from his body. Still, he had to see what it was that had attacked him. Determined, he drew on all his strength to make his way to the foot of the bed.

Before his legs gave out, he looked down to see the old squirrel lying against the baseboard, a small pool of blood gathering beneath her head. He fell to his knees, then to his stomach, his hand releasing its grip on his neck. As his blood flowed onto the carpet, they looked each other in the eyes and time froze.

Nothing existed in either of their worlds at that moment. It was just the two of them, their very souls locked.

She could see the remorse in his eyes, the shock, and the confusion; and in hers, he saw the victory. Together they lay on the warm blood-soaked floor of his bedroom, eyes locked as they drifted off to sleep.

Day Five

Paper Cut

As he entered the doorway of his wife's office in the basement of their 1996 split-foyer home, he swung the black trench coat over his shoulders and asked, "Ready for dinner, hon?"

"I can't. I've got too much to do," she replied without looking up from the contract she was editing. "Tomorrow maybe," crept into his ears as the smile drained from his face. It was a real bitch living with a work-at-home wife who practiced contract law.

"Dammit, Sarah!"

Looking up, she could see the pain in her husband's eyes. "Kevin, I'm sorry. If I break from this I'll have to start all over again. You know how it is."

Crossing his arms, he let out a barely audible "Hmph!"

"Look, pick me up something tonight."

"I pick up your dinner every night."

"Please, Kev? I'll make it up to you. We'll go out tomorrow night."

"Usual story," he said as his eyes began to tear up.

"With a long, drawn-out sigh, she said "Okay. After dinner I'll change into that black negligee you like and we'll have some fun."

"Uh-huh," he said , knowing good and well it wouldn't happen. She would eat dinner, then go back to work for a couple more hours to "tie up the loose ends." After that, she would jump in the shower and head straight for the bed. That was her routine. By the time she was in bed, it was usually around midnight and he was long asleep. Such was the course of events throughout their marriage. Sex only came on her schedule, and at that, it was a bargaining tool. In her world, sex was used to make things better, not for pleasure. He remained steadfastly loyal to her, although he wanted to sleep with every woman he met.

"Kevin, I promise. After dinner we're going to fuck like rabbits. You won't be able to get out of bed in the morning your dick's going to be so sore."

He looked at her, emotionless. "What do you want?"

"I don't know, surprise me."

It hurt her to have to put her work before her husband. She wished she could change careers, but law was all she knew. It was what drove her. Their marriage had grown to be a hollow one. In the beginning, the plan was perfect. She would stay home and run her own practice and he would be free to go off and play. And when it came time to have children, he would take up the role of stay-at-home dad and raise them. Putting children in daycare was something they were bound and determined *not* to do. With Sarah's practice it was possible, but it came at a price neither one of them could easily afford.

"All right," he said, his voice trailing away before he could finish what he was saying.

"Kevin, what do you want from me? This is what..."

"I WANT YOU TO BE MY *FUCKING WIFE!*" he angrily belted out before he slammed the door behind him and stormed out of the room. When he did, the picture of the two of them at their wedding reception on the table by the door fell face down and the ceramic cross hanging above the door fell to the floor and broke in two.

Sarah sat there, stunned, and just stared at the back of the door. "I'm sorry," she said as tears filled her eyes. "I love you, Kevin." Her heart broke at those words and it wasn't until that moment that she realized how much she was hurting *him*. The thought of it never once occurred to her. She was still young, very successful, and had the means to do what she wanted, and it consumed her life. She had allowed her work to become her new love, just as a man allows his work to become his mistress. She realized then that she did, in fact, love her work more than she loved her husband.

She threw her pen across the room, buried her face in her hands, and began to sob. She sobbed like she had never sobbed before. All the frustration and pain that she had allowed to build up inside her came rushing forward, and thoughts of her dear Kevin drowned out all others. She had always been taught to be strong, and strong she was. From her childhood, she'd bottled everything up and kept her emotions to herself. "Oh God, what have I done?"

When the tears stopped flowing, she leaned back in her chair and looked at her desk, disgusted. The papers, the computer, the calculator, the pens and pencils, all suddenly appeared to her as vile instruments used to steal her away from the man she loved. For the first time in her career, she felt hatred beginning to fill her heart. She began to feel contempt for the very thing that she truly loved.

Unable to bear the sight of it any longer, she leaned forward and shoved it all forward, flinging it all off the back of her desk. Her formerly neatly stacked and sorted paperwork scattered haphazardly across the floor. Her monitor fell with a loud crack. The mug shattered into four pieces, and the little container of paper clips spilled its contents, creating a glittering of light across the room. All except the contract, it remained on the desk, teetering over the edge, just far enough so that it would not fall.

She leaned back in her chair, slapping her hands to her forehead. Staring up at the broom-finished ceiling, she took a deep breath to calm herself. The contract sat on the desk, waiting.

Sarah, still leaning back in her chair, started thinking about her life with Kevin, about how wonderful it used to be. She thought about all the good times they had, in the days before law school. She thought about all the hopes and dreams they shared, and where she had messed up. She had never intended for things to work out this way.

During this reflection, she became a woman with a mission. She wanted to make things right with him, to do whatever it took to make their lives as happy as they once were. If it meant cutting her working hours back or taking fewer jobs, she resolved to do it. If it meant actually taking a vacation, she was going to schedule it. If it meant taking off early and making dinner for him, or offering to take over his cleaning duties from time to time, she was going to put on her best Martha Stewart apron and get to work. If it meant giving in to his oft-proclaimed and brushed-off sexual fantasies and blowing him once a day, she was going to suck him for all she was worth.

Resolutions running through her head, she suddenly heard the faint ruffling of paper, as if someone in the room was holding a new ream and fanning it with their thumb. She jolted forward. “Kevin?” she called, but he was nowhere to be seen, and the door was still closed. She leaned back again and was just beginning to calm herself down and think about what she was going to say to him when he got back when she heard the rustling again. Again she looked, but didn't call out to Kevin this time, and still the door was closed.

“Mind must be playing tricks on me.”

It was then that she noticed the contract. There it was, all twenty-three perfectly bound pages, now fully closed and perfectly centered on the surface of the desk. With one eyebrow raised inquisitively, she studied it.

She reached out to touch it, but at the last second pulled her hand back. Something wasn't right. The contract seemed to be calling out to her, and at the same time she felt fear rush through her body. This seemingly harmless stack of legal jargon emitted a power that both intrigued and frightened her.

She felt her hand reaching forward again, slowly, and tried to pull it back. But this time she had no control. The invisible force pulling her hand grew stronger the harder she tried to resist it. Besides her arm, she found herself completely paralyzed. Fear racked her body as she realized she was unable to move. All she wanted to do was run out of this room and go find her Kevin and fall into his arms so he could protect her.

Within inches of the pages, her hand stopped. Her eyes remained locked on it, and she was still unable to move.

"Thwiiiiippp!"

In an instant her reality changed. It was as if an invisible hand had fanned the lower left corner of the contract. Right before her eyes, the corner lifted, bent upward slightly, and all twenty-three pages quickly fell downward onto the sheet beneath.

At once the force released its grip and Sarah recoiled so violently she flipped over in her chair and landed on the floor. She scrambled back to her feet, tripping over the chair and falling once again before becoming sure-footed enough to stand.

She found herself leaning forward with her hands planted firmly on the edge of the desk. When her eyes met the contract, they locked there. Her body froze once again. She had no choice but to stare at the damned stack of paper, every fiber of her being yelling at her to flee. She wanted to, so desperately, but couldn't. The contract held an unrelenting power over her. This contract was evil; she knew it. Knew it to the very marrow of her bones.

"Sarah." Low and hushed, whispering into her ear. With that, the contract slid forward on the desktop toward her. Once again the force relented; she grabbed the paper with both hands and tried to snatch it from its resting place with all her might, intending to fling it across the room to join the rest of the desk's effects on the floor.

It didn't budge. Instead, her hands slid firmly along the sides, the occasional errant sliver of an edge slicing into her dainty fingers, sending a sharp pain through both arms. "Fuck!" Raising her hands to her face, she could see the blood beginning to flow. "Fuck! Fuck! Fuck! Fuck! FUCK!" They were deep.

The bleeding lasted only a minute. The first bit of blood was as red as red could be, but lightening as each second passed. Red, then pink, then clear. As it lightened in color it grew in density and slowed in speed, slower...and slower, until it flowed no more.

"What the...?"

She clasped her hands together. It was sticky, so sticky in fact that she couldn't readily separate them. The ooze created strings between her hands, reflecting the light in droplets from the ceiling light above, reminiscent of sunlight reflecting off the dew on a spider's web in the early morning. It was beautiful. But it also scared the hell out of her.

She was so fascinated with the sticky substance oozing from her palms that she kept pressing them together and pulling them apart again, each time creating more and more of the spider webs, which became even more beautiful. Her fascination drowned out the weakness in her legs.

Her knees buckled and she fell once again to the floor, barely catching herself by her elbows on the edge of the desk. Her eyelids grew heavy and began to flutter, and her equilibrium left her.

With the last bit of energy she could muster, she worked herself back upright and made her way over to the easy chair in the corner of the room. That ten feet felt like five miles; her reserves were completely drained. Her breathing was becoming more and more labored, and she swore she could feel a creak in her knees that hadn't been there before, not in her young, athletic body.

In the chair her joints locked. She could still move her muscles, but the cartilage that cushioned her joints was the first to harden. Yes, first her joints, then her skin. Unable to move yet again, she had no choice but to stare straight ahead at the bookshelf across from her. As her skin hardened, she could see the hair falling from her head through her field of vision, out of view onto her chest and lap below.

Her lungs stopped working. With each passing minute, she could feel things snapping and hear things creaking within her body. Her eyes were the last to go. Her vision faded to black and it was all over. She didn't feel any pain in her death.

Kevin came home just before midnight. "Fucking bitch is still working! Unbelievable!" he exclaimed angrily to himself before shutting off the car and gathering himself to go inside. "This is it. I'm going to go in there. I'm going to...Sarah, I want a divorce." He was left with a lump in his throat after the words left his mouth. He grabbed the little white bag with the cold, hours-old hamburger in it and headed inside.

When he rounded the corner and opened the door, he dropped it in shock. He quickly examined the room, thinking the worst. Divorce quickly left his mind and all thoughts turned to finding Sarah. Papers scattered the floor. The monitor was busted, dangling from the desk by its cabling, and there was a perfectly stacked pile of paper sitting in the middle of the desk.

In the corner of the room, in Sarah's reading chair, a life-sized wood statue of her dressed in her clothes. Its head was bald and its shoulders and chest covered in the same beautiful long red hair that Sarah had.

And a single drop of sap sat in the corner of its left eye.

Day Six

Four (....—)

John sat in the spare bedroom office in the front corner of his little white ranch house, listening to the drone of the low bass notes coming from the teen's car from across the cul-de-sac – or court, if you prefer, if you're English – trying his mightiest to concentrate his whole on the newest chapter of his book. It was Saturday. Wash day.

Saturday was the day the little shit dragged out the hose and washed his car off. All the while, he would leave the stereo on seemingly as loud as it would go. It got even worse when he cleaned the inside. He'd leave the doors wide open and the sound waves would rattle the clock hanging on the office wall. It bothered John so much he adhered a little felt strip to the back side of the clock, but it did no good. It only resulted in a lower tone; the rattling persisted.

Nothing he could do would stop it. He tried ear plugs, but they hurt and were awful inconvenient. And they didn't really work all that well. He tried a pair of sound-deadening ear muffs he used at the firing range. They didn't work either. He even went so far as to add a second layer of drywall to the walls of his office and install better windows, but that didn't work either. The bass frequencies traveled through anything.

Saturday was also the day his wife would leave to visit her mother, allowing him the peace and quiet he needed to work. But, John never got that peace and quiet. The incessant drone from that fucking car was always getting in his head. This really *was* that song you hear on the radio that just won't go away no matter how hard you try.

....— ....— ....—

That pattern – four quick beats followed by one long one – had some kind of meaning, but he couldn't figure out what. The kid would play the same tune over and over again, searing that same pattern into John's brain. Everything John did week after week carried that pattern. When he walked, he would step to that beat. He subconsciously tapped his fingers to it on his desktop. He'd even count to that God-forsaken rhythm.

Week after week for two full years took its toll on him. It drove him crazy, plain and simple. The court took the psychologists' recommendations to heart and gave him a sentence of just ten years. Six years if he behaved himself.

2

"If that little fuck doesn't turn that down, I swear to God I'll..." he said to himself, trying to remain calm.

....— ....— ....—

Same old mantra, same old shit. Maybe one day it'll actually make the jump from "just a word" to full-blown mantra and you'll do something about it, Johnny Boy.

He always wanted more than anything to take drastic measures. The kid's mother refused to do anything about it, always saying "I'll talk to him," whenever John rang the bell and complained. Nothing ever came of it. He had asked the kid several times over the past few months to turn it down out of respect for the other neighbors, politely reminding him that he wasn't the only person living in the neighborhood.

....— ....— ....—

Can you please turn it down?

He called the police last week. As soon as they left, the kid cranked it right back up again. The brief respite only made it seem as if he'd turned it up even louder than it was before.

....— ....— ....—

Morse code, four dots and a dash, was code for the number four. He looked it up in the tiny code book his great grandfather carried in his pocket during his tours with the Navy.

....— *four. It's all connected, man!* Even though it wasn't. Nothing was connected. The state of mind the rhythm put him in made it seem as though everything was. Nothing mattered but *FOUR!* It threw a switch in his head and broke it.

John walked across the street to confront the kid one last time. *I'm gonna teach that little fucker a lesson he'll never forget!*

The kid never heard him coming. When the 17-year-old backed himself out of the passenger side of the car – he had been vacuuming the floorboard – and turned around, he came face to face with his killer.

....— ....— ....—

Eyes locked with John's, he saw the minute movement of the older man's right shoulder and felt a sharp, deep pain in the lower right side of his abdomen.

•

His shoulder moved again. Another sharp pain.

•

Another.

•

And another. This time he stumbled backwards throwing his arms up on the roof behind him for balance.

•

John's eyes met the boy's once more. He slowly smiled, and the kid's eyes widened with fright as he realized what was happening to him.

—

He stood, balancing himself against the car as the blood poured from his abdomen and his small intestine began spilling from the gash across his belly. John stepped back to admire his handiwork, carved across the kid's shirtless gut, just below his little cave of a navel. A perfect **....—** smiled back at him.

3

....— ....— ....—

4

Prison isn't a quiet place. John died on March 7th of this year from repeatedly slamming his face into the wall of his cell in the middle of the night. When the guards found him the next morning, he lay in a pool of blood with a smile on his face.

His wife published the book, *The Sound of Pain,* unfinished, at the request of his will.

Hey, gotta fulfill a man's dying request, right?

Part two of this story, the part you read just before this one, was an excerpt from that very book. She never read it.

....— ....— ....—

Day Seven

Poetry of the Seventh Day

For the seventh day, I thought I would share some old poetry from my late teens. As stated in my Foreword, pay no never-mind to the lack of capitalization or punctuation. I wasn't much for rhyming back then either; what you see is what I felt at the time, thus the way it was written.

Mist

mist
early in the morning
lying on the ground
a sheet of white
like and blanket for the dead
who once walked there
early morning dew lies underneath
cold
like the hand of death

Everyone Laughed

everyone laughed
when i failed
nobody cared
when i prevailed

they all mocked me
when i tried
they all rejoiced
when i cried

they were happy
when i died
it upset them
when i was alive

now i am back
as they grow old
now i am back
to take their souls

Wet Red Lips

my wrists are smiling at me
with their red lips
seeming to laugh at me
yet i cannot hear anything

Take A Bite And Live Forever

open your mind
try to figure out
what it would be like
to die never

tear me open
rip my heart out
take a bite
and live forever

Free Fall

i was falling down
but i never hit the ground
i jumped off the top
to make the pain stop
i felt the wind rush past my face
my body falling free through space
i felt all of my fear
leave my mind as the ground drew near
as my free fall came to an end
i found myself on the roof again

Hold Me Still

hold me still
let me heal
allow these wounds
of mine to seal

let me feel
the hardened steel
salt my wounds
this pain is real

hold me still
let me heal
allow these wounds
of mine to seal

make me cower
be a friend
start all over
do it again

I have more, many more – over two hundred and fifty at the last count, but that was years ago. A book is in the works, but won't be released any time soon. One day I shall oblige.

But I cannot say when.

To the reader:

It has been my pleasure to spin these tales. As this is my first "official" publication as an ink-slinger, you can understand my anxiety. Writing a book, even one as short as this one, has proven to be both a nerve-wracking yet emotionally rewarding experience. I can only hope you enjoyed reading my stories as much as I enjoyed writing them.

Now if you will excuse me, I'm off to start the next one...

www.ingramcontent.com/pod-product-compliance
Lightning Source LLC
LaVergne TN
LVHW050939080826
845145LV00004B/1335

* 9 7 8 0 5 7 8 0 1 9 4 4 4 *